THE DRAGON'S CAPTIVE: THE CLAN BOOK 1

BY:LEA LARSEN

© 2016

DISCLAIMER:

THE INFORMATION PRESENTED IN THIS BOOK REPRESENTS THE VIEWS OF THE PUBLISHER AS OF THE DATE OF PUBLICATION. THE PUBLISHER RESERVES THE RIGHTS TO ALTER UPDATE THEIR OPINIONS BASED ON NEW

CONDITIONS. THIS REPORT IS FOR INFORMATIONAL PURPOSES ONLY. THE AUTHOR AND THE PUBLISHER DO NOT ACCEPT ANY RESPONSIBILITIES FOR ANY LIABILITIES RESULTING FROM THE USE OF THIS INFORMATION. WHILE

EVERY ATTEMPT HAS BEEN MADE TO VERIFY THE INFORMATION PROVIDED HERE, THE AUTHOR AND THE PUBLISHER CANNOT ASSUME ANY RESPONSIBILITY FOR ERRORS, INACCURACIES OR OMISSIONS. ANY SIMILARITIES WITH PEOPLE OR FACTS ARE UNINTENTIONAL.

TABLE OF CONTENTS

Chapter 1 4
Chapter Two 16
Chapter Three 28
Chapter Four 37

Chapter 1

THIS WAS NOT HER SCENE. ALANA MORGAN SAT AT THE BAR AS THE DOZENS OF DRUNK AND SWEATY PATRONS PRESSED IN AROUND HER. GYRATING AND GRINDING TO THE RHYTHM OF ANNOYINGLY MONOTONE CLUB MUSIC THAT MADE IT ALMOST IMPOSSIBLE TO HEAR HERSELF THINK. LET ALONE TALK.

ALANA KNEW SHE SHOULDN'T HAVE COME. BUT, SHE'D HAD NOTHING ELSE TO DO. SHE WAS TIRED OF SITTING IN HER DORMITORY EVERY NIGHT WHILE HER ROOMMATE AND THE OTHER GIRLS FROM HER FLOOR WENT OUT ON THE TOWN. SHE WAS TIRED OF READING BOOKS OR WATCHING MOVIES WHILE EATING FALAFEL OUT OF A SAD, LONELY TAKEOUT CONTAINER.

SO, WHEN HER ROOMMATE SAID THAT IT WAS HER FRIEND'S BIRTHDAY AND A BUNCH OF THEM WERE GOING TO A CLUB CALLED THE DRAGON'S LAIR, ALANA HAD ASKED IF SHE COULD TAG ALONG. NOW, OF COURSE, HER ROOMMATE HAD TAKEN OFF TO DANCE WITH SOME SLEAZY LOOKING GUY FROM THE BAR. THE OTHER GIRLS THEY'D COME WITH HAD DONE THE SAME. AND, ALANA WAS NOW

SITTING AT THE BAR. ALONE.

IF SHE'D KNOWN SHE WAS GOING TO BE FEELING LONELY ANYWAY, SHE WOULD HAVE MADE THE DECISION TO STAY BEHIND IN THE DORMITORY AFTER ALL. AT LEAST THERE SHE HAD FALAFEL AND HER FANTASY BOOKS TO COMFORT HER. HERE, THERE WAS NOTHING. NOTHING BUT AWKWARD LOOKS FROM STRANGERS AND THE OCCASIONAL LEER FROM A DRUNKEN MAN ACROSS THE BAR.

TWO OF THESE GUYS HAD OFFERED TO BUY HER A DRINK AND ONE OF THEM HAD ASKED HER TO DANCE. SHE DECLINED ALL OFFERS. HONESTLY, SHE KNEW SHE SHOULD, AT THE VERY LEAST, MAKE AN EFFORT. BUT, ALL THE MEN WHO SEEMED INTERESTED IN HER GAVE HER A DEFINITE CREEPY, POTENTIAL RAPIST VIBE. NOT TO MENTION, NONE OF THEM WERE HER PHYSICAL TYPE AT ALL.

EVERY MAN WHO HAD COME UP TO HER WERE EITHER THE TYPES WHO WORE BAGGY PANTS, GOLD CHAINS, AND GOLD TEETH OR SPORTED WHAT ALANA CALLED 'THE SERIAL KILLER COMB-OVER'.

NOT THAT THERE WEREN'T GOOD LOOKING GUYS IN THIS CLUB. TRUTH BE TOLD, SHE'D BEEN EYING THE RIPPED REDHEAD ACROSS THE BAR FOR ALMOST AN HOUR. HOPING THAT

HE MIGHT CATCH HER GAZE AND COME OVER.

UNFORTUNATELY, HE SEEMED MORE INTERESTED IN WATCHING HIS COMPANION STRIKE OUT WITH PAIRS OF GIRLS WHO LOOKED, TO ALANA AT LEAST, LIKE SUPER MODELS.

SHE WATCHED THE REDHEAD SMILE SLIGHTLY AS HIS FRIEND, A SHORT, SKINNY GUY WITH LONGISH BROWN HAIR, GET REJECTED BY A COUPLE OF (WHAT ALANA ASSUMED TO BE) BLONDE TWIN SISTERS.

SHE COULDN'T HELP BUT BE AMUSED BY THE LITTLE BROWN HAIRED GUYS ATTEMPTS. CLEARLY HE DIDN'T KNOW THAT THE GIRLS HE WAS GOING AFTER WERE OUT OF HIS LEAGUE.

THAT, ALANA, GUESSED WAS WHY THE CREEPY GUYS WENT FOR HER INSTEAD OF THE SUPERMODELS. THEY FIGURED SHE WAS THE SAFER BET.

NOT THAT SHE WAS BAD LOOKING AT ALL. SHE WAS PROPORTIONAL, OF AVERAGE HEIGHT AND HER BRIGHT BLUE EYES EARNED HER MANY A COMPLIMENT. BUT, WITH A FEW FRECKLES STILL ON HER NOSE (EVEN AT THE AGE OF NINETEEN) AND A TINY HINT OF BABY FAT STILL IN HER CHEEKS, SHE GAVE OFF MORE OF A GIRL-NEXT-DOOR VIBE THAN A

VICTORIA'S SECRET MODEL ONE.
AND, IN HER LIMITED EXPERIENCE WITH CLUBS LIKE THIS ONE, GUYS DIDN'T GO AFTER THE HOTTEST LOOKING GIRL IN THE PLACE. THEY WENT AFTER THE BEST-LOOKING GIRL THEY THOUGHT THEY HAD A CHANCE WITH.

BUT MEN LIKE THE REDHEAD, WITH HIS ON POINT HAIR CUT, CHISELED FEATURES, AND WELL-DEFINED ABS, WHICH WERE DISPLAYED NICELY IN HIS TOO TIGHT WHITE SHIRT, COULD GET ANY GIRL THEY WANTED. ALANA WAS SURE THAT, IF HE TRIED, HE COULD HAVE THE GIRLS HIS LITTLE FRIEND WAS GOING AFTER EATING OUT OF THE PALM OF HIS HAND. DESPITE THAT, HE SEEMED COMPLETELY UNINTERESTED.

ALANA COULDN'T HELP BUT WONDER WHY THAT WAS. SHE SIPPED ON THE SOUTHERN COMFORT SHE HAD ORDERED AND LEANED OVER TO WATCH HIM A BIT MORE CLOSELY. WHEN HE TURNED HIS EYES TO HER, SHE FELT AN EMBARRASSING FLUSH CREEP UP HER FACE. HER MIND BEGAN TO FRANTICALLY SEARCH FOR OTHER PLACES TO LOOK. PLACES THAT WOULD MAKE IT LOOK LIKE SHE WASN'T STARING AT HIM.

THEN HE SMILED AT HER. HER HEART STARTED POUNDING IN HER CHEST AS HE RAISED HIS DRINK IN HER DIRECTION. SHE FELT it speed up as she watched him stand from his stool and make his way around the bar.

When he stopped in front of her, she found that she could hardly breathe.

"Hi," he said loudly over the music. "Can I buy you another?"

She looked at his hypnotic smile and tried her best to smile back as she cleared her throat.

"Su-sure," she managed to stammer. "What are you drinking?" he asked. She could hear a Welsh strain in his voice now. Not unusual, seeing as they were in Wales. But, with a nation this small, and the Cardiff University so close, you heard all sorts of accents in clubs like this one.

"Southern Comfort," she said. He gave a little chuckle.

"Fitting," he said.

"Why?" she asked.

"Well, you're American, aren't you?" he asked.

"HOW'D YOU GUESS?" SHE ASKED SARCASTICALLY. SHE WAS USED TO BEING ASKED ABOUT HER ACCENT. FROM CREEPY GUYS TELLING HER IT WAS HOT TO PEOPLE WANTING TO KNOW WHETHER OR NOT IT WAS TRUE THAT EVERYONE OWNED A GUN IN THE STATES, BRITS SEEMED FASCINATED WITH HER NATION OF ORIGIN.

"I GUESS I HAVE AN EAR FOR THAT KIND OF THING," HE SAID DRYLY. THEN, HE TURNED TOWARDS THE BAR AND SIGNALED THE BARTENDER OVER. AS HE ORDERED HER ANOTHER DRINK, ALANA COULDN'T HELP BUT STARE AT HIM A LITTLE LONGER.

HE WAS TALL. AT LEAST A FEW INCHES ABOVE THE REST OF THE MEN AT THE CLUB. HIS SHOCKING RED HAIR AND NICELY TONED BODY DID INDEED MAKE HIM STAND OUT. AND, AS SHE WATCHED HIM FROM THE BAR, ALANA CAUGHT A VERY NICE VIEW FROM BEHIND. THAT WAS MORE THAN IMPRESSIVE AS WELL.

SHE SUDDENLY FELT SLIGHTLY FLUSHED AGAIN AS A SENSATION WASHED OVER HER THAT SHE HADN'T EXPERIENCED IN A LONG TIME.

THE BARTENDER SLID THE DRINK ACROSS THE BAR TO THE REDHEAD AND HE CAUGHT IT DEFTLY. HE TURNED TO ALANA AND GAVE HER

A SMILE THAT CAUSED HER TO MELT FROM THE INSIDE OUT LIKE THE CHOCOLATE IN THE MIDDLE OF A S'MORE.

SHE SWALLOWED AND TRIED HER BEST TO SMILE BACK AT HIM IN THE COOL CONFIDENT WAY SHE'D SEEN OTHER GIRLS AT THE BAR SMILE AT MEN. IN THE END, SHE WAS AFRAID THE LOOK CAME OFF A BIT PATHETIC. IF IT DID, THE REDHEAD DIDN'T SEEM PHASED.
"SO," HE SAID. "HOW DOES A NICE AMERICAN GIRL LIKE YOU END UP IN A DINGY CLUB IN WALES?"

"REALLY?" SHE COULDN'T HELP BUT ASK. "THAT'S YOUR LINE?"

"WHO SAID ANYTHING ABOUT A LINE?" HE ASKED. "MAYBE I REALLY WANT TO KNOW."

"THAT'S WHY GUYS BUY GIRLS DRINKS, RIGHT?" SHE ASKED. "BECAUSE YOU WANT TO GET TO KNOW THEM?"

MAYBE SHE WAS BEING TOO DEFENSIVE. BUT SOME HORRIBLE PART IN THE BACK OF HER MIND KEPT WAITING FOR SOME SORT OF CATCH. GUYS AS GOOD LOOKING AS THIS ONE SIMPLY DIDN'T HIT ON HER. SHE FOUND HERSELF AT AN ALMOST COMPLETE LOSS FOR HOW TO BEHAVE AND, WHEN THAT HAPPENED, DEFENSIVENESS BECAME HER DEFAULT

POSITION.
THE REDHEAD ONCE AGAIN IMPRESSED HER BY LAUGHING INSTEAD OF BECOMING DEFENSIVE RIGHT BACK.

"OK," HE SAID, A NOTE OF AMUSEMENT STILL LINING HIS VOICE. "YOU CAUGHT ME.

AND, SINCE MY LINE DIDN'T WORK. HOW ABOUT WE START WITH NAMES? I'M LLEWELLYN. YOU CAN CALL ME LLEW."

"ALANA," SHE SAID SIMPLY.

"ALANA," HE ECHOED WITH ANOTHER SMILE THAT CAUSED A MELTING SENSATION TO RUSH THROUGH HER STOMACH. "NICE TO MEET YOU."

WITH WHAT SHE HOPED WAS A SECRETIVE SMILE, SHE TURNED AWAY SLIGHTLY AND SIPPED AT THE DRINK HE HAD GIVEN HER. ADMITTEDLY, AS THIS WAS HER SECOND, HER HEAD WAS STARTING TO FEEL PLEASANTLY DIZZY.

"NOW THAT WE'VE GOT THE INTRODUCTIONS OUT OF THE WAY," HE SAID. "MAYBE YOU'LL BE A LITTLE MORE RECEPTIVE TO MY QUESTION?"
"THE ONE ABOUT HOW I ENDED UP HERE?" SHE ASKED. "IT'S NOT VERY INTERESTING."

"I DOUBT THAT," HE SAID.

"I'M STUDYING AT THE UNIVERSITY IN CARDIFF," SHE SAID. "SOME OF THE GIRLS IN MY DORM WERE COMING HERE TONIGHT AND I DECIDED TO TAG ALONG."

APPARENTLY HER ATTEMPT TO HIDE THE REGRET IN HER VOICE HAD FAILED. BECAUSE HIS SMILE DIMMED SLIGHTLY AND HE SCOOTED A LITTLE CLOSER TO HER.

"I TAKE IT THIS WASN'T YOUR FIRST CHOICE TO SPEND THE EVENING," HE SAID.

"I THOUGHT IT WOULD BE GOOD TO ACTUALLY GET OUT," ALANA SAID. "TURNS OUT I'D RATHER BE BACK IN MY ROOM RE-READING FELLOWSHIP OF THE RING."

"I'LL TRY NOT TO TAKE THAT PERSONALLY," HE SAID.

"DON'T," SHE TOLD HIM. "IT'S NOT YOU. I'M JUST NOT VERY SOCIAL."

"TO TELL THE TRUTH, I'M NOT EITHER," HE SAID. "THIS WHOLE THING WAS MY BROTHER'S IDEA."
LLEW NODDED HIS HEAD TOWARDS THE SMALL, BROWN-HAIRED GUY ACROSS THE BAR

who was engaged in another unsuccessful pickup attempt. This time, it was an elegant looking girl with long dark hair and a permanent pout on her lips.

"I wouldn't say no to being curled up in my bed reading some Tolkien right now either," he said.

Alana tried to ignore the flush that rushed through her at the thought of this man in her bed. Instead, she tried to focus on the second part of his comment. Though, trying to focus on anything was becoming increasingly difficult. Her head was feeling fuzzier by the minute and the world around her had become slightly blurred.

"I wouldn't have taken you for a Tolkien fan," she said, trying to force the increasingly fuzzy sensation away.

"Never judge a book by its cover," he quipped.

They continued to talk about the Tolkien trilogy as well as several other fantasy books that Alana had lately been taken with. She was surprised to learn that Llew had read

QUITE A FEW OF THEM AND THE ONES HE HADN'T HE SEEMED VERY INTERESTED IN LEARNING ABOUT. ALANA WAS HALF CONVINCED THAT SHE WAS FALLING IN LOVE.

STILL, SHE COULD NOT BE SURE IF THAT WAS BECAUSE OF LLEWELLYN OR THE FALLING SENSATION SHE WAS BEGINNING TO EXPERIENCE AS A RESULT OF THE ALCOHOL.

THOUGH, REALLY, SHE WAS CERTAIN SHE HAD NEVER FELT QUITE THIS UNSTABLE AFTER TWO DRINKS.

BY THE TIME LLEW'S BROTHER MADE HIS WAY OVER TO THEM, ALANA WAS FIGHTING TO KEEP HERSELF STANDING STRAIGHT UP. SHE WAS JUST COGNIZANT ENOUGH TO CATCH THE WORDS LLEW AND HIS BROTHER WERE SPEAKING TO EACH OTHER.

"WHAT ARE YOU DOING?" LLEW'S BROTHER ASKED GESTURING FIERCELY TO ALANA.

"WHAT DOES IT LOOK LIKE I'M DOING?" LLEW SAID IN AN UNDERTONE.

"JUST...PLEASE TELL ME YOU DIDN'T MARK HER," THE BROTHER SAID, SOUNDING EXASPERATED. ALANA SQUINTED AS SHE TRIED TO MOVE TOWARDS THE BROTHERS. SHE WAS NOW POSITIVE THAT WHAT SHE WAS

FEELING WASN'T NORMAL DRUNKENNESS. AND SHE NEEDED TO KNOW EXACTLY WHAT "MARKED" MEANT.

"WHAT-WHAT DID YOU…?" SHE FELT HER LEGS COLLAPSE BENEATH HER AS SHE GRABBED A HOLD OF LLEW'S ARM FOR SUPPORT. HE TURNED TO HER AND STARED DIRECTLY INTO HER EYES.

"ALANA, JUST KEEP FOCUSED ON ME," HE SAID URGENTLY. "EVERYTHING WILL BE ALL RIGHT. I PROMISE."

ALANA COULD DO LITTLE BUT WHAT SHE WAS TOLD. SHE KEPT HER EYES FOCUSED COMPLETELY ON HIS. AS SHE DID, HIS GREEN EYES SHINED DOWN AT HER AND, THROUGH A DIZZY HAZE, SHE WAS SURE SHE SAW SOMETHING DIFFERENT, SOMETHING INTRIGUING IN THEM.

THE LONGER SHE STARED THE MORE THEY SEEMED TO FLASH, ALMOST TO MOVE. LIKE THE SCALES OF A GREAT ANIMAL.

THOSE STRANGE, MOVING EYES WERE THE LAST THINGS SHE SAW BEFORE THE WORLD AROUND HER FADED FROM VIEW.

Chapter Two

"AN AREFOL! HE BROUGHT AN AREFOL TO OUR CARTREF!"

ALANA COULD HEAR VOICES ABOVE HER. HER HEAD WAS LAYING ON SOMETHING SOFT. A PILLOW. AND SHE FELT SHEETS CURLED AROUND HER BODY. CLEARLY, SHE HAD BEEN TAKEN SOMEWHERE.

THE VOICE THAT HAD SPOKEN WAS ONE SHE RECOGNIZED, BUT ONLY DIMLY. THE NEXT VOICE WAS MUCH MORE FAMILIAR.

"THE TEXTS DIDN'T SPECIFY THAT THE GIRL NEEDED TO BE A DRAIG," LLEW SAID. "NOR DID FATHER BEFORE HE DIED. ALL HE SAID WAS THAT WE NEEDED TO FIND A GIRL. TWO IF POSSIBLE. AND, NOW, WE'VE FOUND ONE."

ALANA KEPT HER EYES PRESSED CLOSED HOPING THAT, WHILE THEY THOUGHT SHE WAS UNCONSCIOUS, THEY WOULD EXPLAIN EXACTLY WHAT THEY INTENDED TO DO WITH HER. SHE'D BEEN KIDNAPPED, THAT WAS CLEAR. BUT, SHE STILL HAD NO IDEA WHY. AND, WHAT'S MORE, SHE HAD NO IDEA WHAT THESE STRANGE WORDS THEY WERE USING

MEANT.

She thought the words, Arefol, Cartref, sounded Welsh. She'd become fairly familiar with the language after six months studying there. At the very least, she knew it when she heard it spoken. But, she'd no idea what they meant. Or what they had to do with her.

"Regardless," a new female voice said. "Now that the girl is here, she can not be allowed to leave. If she did, we would risk exposure or worse." This voice was deep, clear and authoritative. Clearly, the woman was the leader here.

The first voice, which Alana realized belonged to Llew's brother, cursed to the room.

"All is not lost, Owain," the woman said. "We've needed a consort for the men in the clan for years. There are few women now. Those eligible have already been mated. Our young men need someone to express their...urges with. An Arefol girl will do."

Alana felt her blood freeze. Though she still had no idea what Arefol meant or what the clan was, it was now clear

WHAT THEY MEANT TO DO WITH HER. THEY WANTED TO MAKE HER A SEX SLAVE. A SEX SLAVE FOR SOME...WEIRD...CULT.

SHE FOUGHT, DESPERATELY AGAINST THE URGE TO OPEN HER EYES, JUMP FROM THE BED AND TRY TO RUSH OUT OF...WHEREVER SHE WAS. SHE REALIZED THAT SHE WOULD NEED TO GET OUT OF THIS. AND, IF SHE WAS GOING TO, SHE WOULD NEED TO FIND OUT EVERYTHING SHE COULD. ABOUT WHO THESE PEOPLE WERE, WHERE SHE WAS AND WHAT EXACTLY THEY WERE PLANNING TO DO.

"THAT'S NOT THE ONLY OPTION," LLEW SAID FIRMLY.

"WE KNOW YOUR THEORY, LLEW," OWAIN CUT IN. "DON'T—"

"LET YOUR BROTHER SPEAK, OWAIN," THE WOMAN SAID FIERCELY. "REMEMBER, NOW THAT YOUR FATHER HAS PASSED, LLEWELLYN WILL BECOME THE CLAN LEADER."

EVEN WITH HER EYES CLOSED, ALANA COULD SENSE THE TENSION IN THE SILENCE THAT PASSED BETWEEN THE THREE PEOPLE ABOVE HER.

"YES MOTHER," OWAIN SAID FINALLY. THOUGH, THERE WAS A DEFINITE BITTER NOTE

TO HIS VOICE.

"THE GIRL IS A VIRGIN, I'M SURE OF IT," LLEW SAID. ALANA FELT THE BLOOD RUSH TOWARDS HER FACE AND PRAYED THAT HER BLUSH WASN'T NOTICEABLE. HOW HE HAD KNOWN ABOUT HER SEXUAL INEXPERIENCE WAS QUITE BEYOND HER.

"THE TEXTS SAY THAT A LEADER MAY CHOOSE A VIRGIN GIRL FOR HIS MATE. IT DOES NOT SPECIFY WHETHER THAT GIRL SHOULD BE A DRAIG OR AN AREFOL."

"NO ONE IN THE CLAN HAS EVER BEEN MATED TO AN AREFOL," OWAIN SAID. "IT WOULD BE NEAR TO BLASPHEMY FOR A LEADER TO DO SO."

"WHY?" LLEW ASKED FIERCELY. "THE TEXTS DON'T SAY—"

"THINK ABOUT IT, LLEW!" OWAIN SAID. "CHILDREN BORN FROM AN AREFOL AND A DRAIG UNION MIGHT NOT EVEN SURVIVE. AND IF THEY DO, NO ONE KNOWS WHAT ABILITIES THEY WILL HAVE IF ANY AT ALL."

"SO THE OPTION IS TO CONTINUE MARRYING WITHIN THE CLAN?" LLEW ASKED. "KEEP ON MARRYING COUSINS UNTIL OUR PEOPLE DIE OUT ENTIRELY? WE ALREADY

HAVE A SHORTAGE OF WOMEN. NEW BLOOD IS NEEDED—"

"NOT NEW AREFOL BLOOD!" OWAIN INSISTED.

"ENOUGH!" THEIR MOTHER INSISTED. THE BOYS STOPPED THEIR BICKERING IMMEDIATELY.

"THERE ARE STILL FOUR WEEKS UNTIL LLEWELLYN'S CORONATION. WE WILL KEEP THE GIRL HERE UNTIL THEN. ON THE DAY OF THE FULL MOON, HE WILL DECIDE WHAT IS BEST TO DO."

"BUT MOTHER—" OWAIN BEGAN.

"HE WILL BE THE CLAN LEADER," THE MOTHER SAID. "IT IS HIS DECISION. I ONLY HOPE YOU CONSIDER IT CAREFULLY, LLEWELLYN. THERE IS TOO MUCH AT STAKE FOR OUR FAMILY TO GAMBLE OUR FUTURE BECAUSE OF YOUR PASSION FOR A PRETTY AREFOL GIRL."

THERE WAS A BRIEF SILENCE. NOT QUITE AS TENSE AS THE ONE THAT PRECEDED IT BUT STILL PREGNANT WITH MEANING.

"OF COURSE, MOTHER," LLEWELLYN SAID.

"THAT IS SETTLED THEN," THE MOTHER SAID. "OWAIN AND I WILL LEAVE YOU NOW."

ALANA LISTENED TO THE FOOTSTEPS AS THE MOTHER AND OWAIN WALKED AWAY FROM HER BED. A TELLTALE CLICK OF THE DOOR TOLD HER THAT THEY HAD LEFT THE ROOM.

NOW THAT THEY WERE GONE, ALANA TOOK A CHANCE AND OPENED HER EYES. WHEN SHE DID, SHE SAW THOSE GREEN EYES STARING BACK AT HER. THEY LOOKED EVERY BIT AS FIERY AND ALIVE AS THEY HAD IN THE CLUB. JUST BEFORE SHE HAD FALLEN TO THE STICKY FLOOR.

"WHERE AM I?" ALANA ASKED.

"SAFE. THAT'S ALL YOU NEED TO KNOW," HE SAID. "FOR NOW."

"WHY DID YOU BRING ME HERE?" SHE ASKED.

"IT'S COMPLICATED," HE TOLD HER. "AND YOU'RE IN NO STATE TO UNDERSTAND IT NOW."

"YEAH," ALANA ANSWERED FIERCELY. "I GUESS BEING SLIPPED A DATE RAPE DRUG WILL DO THAT TO YOU."

NOW, AS THE FEAR WAS DISSIPATING, A SWELL OF ANGER BEGAN TO RISE UP TO HER CHEST AND MINGLE WITH THE ANXIETY FILLED BEATS OF HER HEART.

"I'M SORRY I HAD TO TRICK YOU," HE SAID. THOUGH HE SOUNDED GENUINE, ALANA FORCED HERSELF NOT TO BE MOVED. HER ARMS REMAINED FOLDED ACROSS HER CHEST AND HER EYES FOCUSED ON HIM GLARING DARKLY.

"BELIEVE ME, I WOULDN'T HAVE IF THERE WAS ANY OTHER WAY," HE SAID.

"ANOTHER WAY TO DO WHAT, EXACTLY?" ALANA ASKED. SHE KEPT THE FIERCENESS IN HER VOICE AS SHE TOOK STOCK OF THE ROOM SHE WAS IN. IT WAS GIGANTIC BY ANY STANDARDS. MORE OF AN APARTMENT THAN A BEDROOM. SHE COULD SEE A CANOPY ABOVE HER BED, A CLOSET TO HER RIGHT. THERE WAS A COMFORTABLE LOOKING COUCH JUST UNDERNEATH A TALL, LARGE WINDOW. AND, JUST TO THE SIDE OF THAT, LOOKED LIKE HER ONLY MEANS OF ESCAPE. A DOOR.

"AS I SAID," LLEW TOLD HER. "I'LL EXPLAIN IT TO YOU AS SOON AS I CAN. FOR NOW, YOU MUST STAY IN THIS ROOM."

"LIKE HELL!" SHE SAID. "YOU CAN'T MAKE ME STAY HERE. PEOPLE WILL NOTICE IF I DISAPPEAR—"

"WE BOTH KNOW THAT'S NOT TRUE," LLEWELLYN SAID. ALANA FELT HER FACE GO PALE. SHE WANTED TO ASK HOW HE KNEW. HOW HE COULD TELL THAT SHE WAS BLUFFING. BUT, SHE HAD A FEELING HE KNEW THE SAME WAY HE HAD DISCOVERED SHE WAS A VIRGIN.

CLEARLY, HE KNEW ABOUT HER PAST. HE KNEW THAT HER PARENTS HAD BEEN KILLED IN A CAR WRECK FIVE YEARS AGO. KNEW THAT THE AUNT AND UNCLE SHE'D GONE TO LIVE WITH IN LONDON HAD LITTLE TIME FOR HER. KNEW THAT SHE HAD YET TO MAKE ANY FRIENDS AT HER UNIVERSITY.

HE WAS RIGHT. NO ONE WOULD NOTICE OR CARE IF SHE DISAPPEARED FROM THE FACE OF THE EARTH.

SHE LET THAT DEPRESSING THOUGHT SINK IN BEFORE STRAIGHTENING HERSELF UP AND TRYING ANOTHER TACTIC.

"WILL YOU AT LEAST TELL ME WHY I WON'T BE ALLOWED OUT OF THIS ROOM?" SHE ASKED FOLDING HER ARMS ACROSS HER CHEST. LLEWELLYN HEAVED ANOTHER SIGH AND PUT

HIS HAND ON THE BEDPOST AS HE TURNED BACK TO HER.

"FOR NOW, SUFFICE IT TO SAY, THERE ARE...PEOPLE HERE WHO WILL NOT BE SO KIND TO YOU IF YOU STEP OUT ALONE."

HE LOOKED AT HER WITH AN EXPRESSION THAT WAS WELL BEYOND SERIOUS. WHEN HIS EYES LOOKED INTO HERS, IT WAS AS THOUGH HER STAYING HERE, IN THIS ROOM WAS A MATTER OF LIFE AND DEATH. THE EXPRESSION FORCED THE FEAR BACK INTO ALANA'S LIMBS AND SHE FELT HER HEART BEGIN TO POUND IN A FIERCE AND QUICK RHYTHM.

"WHAT SORT OF PEOPLE?" SHE ASKED QUIETLY.

"YOU'LL SEE, EVENTUALLY," HE ANSWERED. "FOR NOW, PLEASE GET SOME REST."

SHE STARED AT HIM A LONG WHILE, HER ARMS STILL CROSSED BEFORE DECIDING THAT NOW, WHEN SHE WAS ALONE WITH LLEW, WAS HER BEST CHANCE TO GET OUT OF THE ROOM. TO SEE WHAT WAS REALLY GOING ON.

"AND WHAT IF I WANT TO SEE NOW?" SHE ASKED.

BEFORE HE COULD SAY ANYTHING MORE, SHE STOOD FROM THE BED AND MARCHED PURPOSEFULLY TOWARDS THE DOOR. SHE HAD BARELY MADE IT TWO FEET BEFORE A SOFT, YET FIRM HAND GRABBED HOLD OF HER WRIST AND PULLED HER BACK.

WHEN SHE LOOKED BACK AT LLEWELLYN, HIS EYES WERE DESPERATE, ALMOST FEARFUL. THAT CAUSED HER HEART TO BEAT EVEN MORE QUICKLY.

"ALANA, PLEASE," HE SAID. "YOU MUST PROMISE ME YOU WILL NEVER GO OUT THERE ALONE."

"WHAT WILL HAPPEN IF I DO?" SHE ASKED QUIETLY.

"JUST PROMISE ME."

BOTH HIS HANDS WERE CLUTCHED OVER HERS NOW AND THE PLEADING EXPRESSION ON HIS FACE WAS MORE THAN PALPABLE.

"FINE," SHE SAID RELUCTANTLY. "I PROMISE."

"GOOD," HE ANSWERED BREATHING A SIGH OF RELIEF. HE LED HER BACK TO THE BED AND LAID HER DOWN UNDERNEATH THE SHEETS. WHEN HE MOVED THE BLANKETS AROUND her, she realized that this was the first time in a long time anyone had tucked her in.

When his warm hand brushed against her shoulder, a sharp, pleasant shiver ran through her body. That had certainly never happened when her parents used to put her to bed.

"Breakfast will be brought up to you in the morning," he said. "As well as some new clothes."

She looked up at him and tried to speak, but, no words seemed able to form in her mouth. She nodded her understanding instead. She was almost glad to see his expression soften when she did.

Alana held her breath as Llewellyn leaned over her, bent down and placed a gentle, lingering kiss on her forehead.

"Goodnight, Alana," he whispered, pulling back.
She tried to say good night as well, tried to express some sort of acknowledgment. But, when she looked into his green eyes, she found that, once again, words failed her. Instead, she

NODDED ONCE MORE.

HE BACKED AWAY FROM THE BED, KEEPING HIS EYES FIXED ON HER UNTIL HE REACHED THE DOOR OF THE ROOM AND TURNED OUT THE LIGHT.

AS ALANA TURNED TO SLEEP, SHE FOUND THAT THE LAST THOUGHTS SHE HAD WERE OF LLEWELLYN AND THE KISS THAT STILL SEARED ON HER FOREHEAD LIKE A BRAND.

Chapter Three

WHEN SHE WOKE THAT MORNING, AS PROMISED, BREAKFAST STOOD READY FOR HER BY HER BEDSIDE. TWO EGGS OVER EASY, SAUSAGE, BAKED BEANS, A FRIED TOMATO AND TOAST ALONG WITH COFFEE. IT WAS A MUCH LARGER MEAL THAN SHE HAD EVER DARED TO EAT IN THE MORNING BEFORE. BUT, SHE GOT THE FEELING THAT THESE PEOPLE, WHOEVER THEY WERE, WERE VERY TRADITIONAL. AND THIS WAS WHAT THEY CALLED A TRADITIONAL FULL WELSH BREAKFAST.

AS SHE PUT HER FEET ON THE FLOOR AND MADE TO GRASP FOR A SLICE OF TOAST, A SMALL PIECE OF PAPER CAUGHT HER EYE. SHE GRASPED IT AND UNFOLDED IT TO FIND A NOTE IN NEAT, CURSIVE HANDWRITING.

ALANA, IT BEGAN.
I HOPE YOU ARE FEELING BETTER THIS MORNING. THERE ARE FRESH CLOTHES FOR YOU IN THE WARDROBE. THE LOO IS IN THE ROOM JUST TO THE RIGHT SIDE OF THE BED. THERE'S A SHOWER AND BATH IN THERE SO THAT YOU CAN GET CLEANED UP. ALSO, I'VE HAD THEM PLACE A

SMALL GIFT FOR YOU ON THE BOOKSHELVES BESIDE THE WINDOW. THINK OF IT AS MY WAY OF SAYING "SORRY". I EXPECT I'LL SEE YOU SOON.
-LLEW

WITH THE NOTE READ, ALANA STILL TRIED AS HARD AS SHE COULD TO BE ANGRY WITH HIM. HOW COULD SHE NOT BE ANGRY WITH A MAN WHO HAD SLIPPED HER A ROOFIE AND KIDNAPPED HER? BUT, WHEN SHE LOOKED DOWN AT THIS DELICIOUS SMELLING BREAKFAST AND THOUGHT OF THE TROUBLE HE HAD OBVIOUSLY GONE TO HAVE CLOTHES PLACED FOR HER AND EVEN A GIFT, IT WAS BECOMING MORE AND MORE DIFFICULT TO STAY MAD.

THE GIFT PIQUED HER CURIOSITY MORE THAN ANYTHING ELSE. SETTING HER TOAST DOWN AND HER FEET ON THE FLOOR, SHE PADDED HER WAY OVER TO THE BOOKSHELF. THERE, SHE COULD NOT HELP THE SMILE THAT CROSSED HER FACE.

THE LARGE STRUCTURE, WITH FOUR SHELVES FULL OF ANTIQUE, BEAUTIFULLY BOUND BOOKS, SEEMED TO CONTAIN EVERY VOLUME SHE HAD MENTIONED TO LLEWELLYN THE NIGHT BEFORE. TOLKIEN'S ENTIRE LIBRARY WAS THERE AS WELL AS C.S. LEWIS, JK ROWLING, NEIL GAIMAN AND A FEW OTHERS THAT SHE DID NOT KNOW BUT SOUNDED PROMISING.

She dressed and washed as quickly as she could. The clothing was just as impressive as the books had been, though less interesting to Alana. Dresses of varying lengths that were made of fine silk and beautiful linens hung in her wardrobe. She picked out the simplest of these, a pale blue sundress.

Once she was dressed, she rushed over to the books and immediately selected one of the newer ones which she was anxious to read. She settled herself on the window seat and, looking out, was immediately distracted by a beautiful, ruined stone castle.

The tower was still intact and stood with its pure white stones gleaming against the morning sun. The rest of the structure was moss colored and faded by time. It looked very much like the sort of thing one might come across in a fantasy novel and Alana found herself anxious to explore it.
But, then she remembered Llewellyn's warning.

The pleading look that had laced his eyes the night before. She knew that,

WHATEVER WAS OUT THERE, IT FRIGHTENED HIM. AND, IF A MAN AS TOUGH AS LLEWELLYN SEEMED TO BE WAS FRIGHTENED, THERE WAS MOST LIKELY, GOOD REASON FOR IT.

SO, SHE TRIED HER BEST TO IGNORE THE CASTLE IN FAVOR OF HER BOOKS. IT WASN'T UNTIL JUST BEFORE NOON THAT MOVEMENT FROM THE GROUND BELOW CAUGHT HER EYE. SHE LOOKED DOWN TO SEE THAT A SMALL GROUP OF YOUNG MEN WERE MAKING THEIR WAY TOWARDS THE RUINED CASTLE. AND, WHAT'S MORE, THE YOUNG MEN WERE SHIRTLESS.

ALANA GAVE INTO HER BASE URGE AND SET THE BOOK SHE WAS READING ASIDE, DECIDING INSTEAD, TO WATCH THESE FIT YOUNG MEN.

ALL OF THEM WERE MUSCULAR. SOME WERE WELL-TANNED OTHERS WERE PALER. THEY ALL SEEMED TO SHARE A MATCHING RED TATTOO EMBLAZONED ACROSS THEIR BACKS. FROM A DISTANCE, IT LOOKED LIKE SOME SORT OF GREAT SNAKE.

SOME HAD FAIR HAIR SOME HAD DARK. THERE WAS ONLY ONE HEAD OF SHOCKING RED HAIR IN THE GROUP. THAT BELONGED TO LLEWELLYN. HIS TORSO WAS ONE OF THE ONES THAT WERE FAIRER THAN THE OTHERS.

STILL, THE GLEAM OF SUNLIGHT ON HIS MUSCULAR FRAME CAUSED A TINGLING SENSATION TO RUSH THROUGH ALANA'S CHEST AND STRAIGHT DOWN TO HER CORE.

SHE WATCHED AS THE MEN GATHERED IN A CIRCLE. APPARENTLY, PERFORMING SOME SORT OF RITUAL. SHE COULD BARELY MAKE OUT LLEWELLYN BEGINNING TO SPEAK TO THE GROUP. SHE WISHED DESPERATELY THAT SHE COULD HEAR THE WORDS BEING SAID.

THAT WAS WHEN AN IDEA HIT HER. SHE COULD HEAR THE WORDS. AFTER ALL, LLEWELLYN HAD NOT FORBIDDEN HER FROM LEAVING THE ROOM ENTIRELY, JUST FROM LEAVING THE ROOM ALONE. THE CASTLE WAS MERE FEET FROM THE SIDE OF THE HOUSE WHERE HER BEDROOM SAT AND, ONCE SHE REACHED THE CASTLE, SHE WOULD NOT BE ALONE AT ALL. LLEWELLYN WOULD BE THERE.

HER MIND MADE UP, SHE OPENED THE BEDROOM DOOR AND RUSHED DOWN THE STAIRS JUST TO THE RIGHT OF IT. WHEN SHE REACHED THE OUTSIDE DOOR, SHE PULLED IT OPEN AS QUIETLY AS SHE COULD AND MADE HER WAY OUTSIDE.

THE SOUND OF CHANTING FILLED THE AIR AS ALANA FOUND A SHRUB NEAR THE CASTLE LARGE ENOUGH TO HIDE BEHIND. FROM THERE,

SHE COULD SEE THE MEN THROUGH THE RUINED STONE AS THEY CHANTED THEIR STRANGE MELODY.

IT WAS WELSH, SHE KNEW THAT MUCH, THOUGH SHE COULD NOT MAKE OUT THE WORDS. THE MELODY FELT ANCIENT, AS THOUGH IT MIGHT HAVE BEEN CREATED CENTURIES BEFORE.

SUDDENLY, THE VOICES STOPPED COMPLETELY. SHE WATCHED AS EACH OF THE MEN CLOSED HIS EYES IN TURN. THEY GRASPED HANDS AND, IN UNISON, LET OUT A GREAT YELL THAT ECHOED ALONG THE GREEN CLIFFS OF THE LANDSCAPE.

ALANA SCREAMED AND SHOT BACKWARD AS THE MEN BEFORE HER EACH DISAPPEARED TO BE REPLACED BY LARGE, RED DRAGONS.

THE CREATURES, APPARENTLY OBLIVIOUS TO HER, TOOK THE SKY AND BEGAN TO SOAR GRACEFULLY ABOVE THE RUINED CASTLE AND CLIFFS AND TREES.

ALANA'S FEET WERE LIKE LEAD. HEAVY AND FROZEN TO THE SPOT WHERE SHE STOOD. SHE COULD FEEL HER HEART THUMPING INSIDE HER CHEST AS THOUGH IT MIGHT EXPLODE. SHE KEPT HER EYES ON THE DRAGONS CIRCLING ABOVE THE CASTLE AND GASPED AGAIN AS ONE TOOK A BEAUTIFUL AND SMOOTH DIVE OFF THE CLIFF ON WHICH THE HOUSE AND CASTLE STOOD.

WITHOUT BEING AWARE OF MOVING HER FEET, ALANA STEPPED OUT OF THE BUSHES AND MADE TO MOVE TOWARDS THE PLACE WHERE THE DIVING DRAGON HAD DISAPPEARED.

AS SOON AS SHE DID, ANOTHER DRAGON OUT OF THE CORNER OF HER EYE CAUGHT HER ATTENTION. WHEN SHE TURNED TOWARDS IT, SHE REALIZED IT WAS FLYING STRAIGHT TOWARDS HER. ITS FACE SET IN APPARENT MALEVOLENCE, SMOKE RISING MENACINGLY FROM ITS NOSTRILS.

THERE WAS NO QUESTION NOW. THE CREATURE HAD SEEN HER.

Chapter Four

WITH ANOTHER SCREAM, ALANA THREW HERSELF TO THE GROUND. SHE BARELY FELT THE ROCK ON WHICH SHE HAD LANDED HIT AND CUT HER CHEEK BEFORE SHE SCREAMED AGAIN.

HUGE TALONS WERE CLOSING IN ON HER, MOVING OVER HER LIKE A CAT CATCHING A MOUSE BENEATH ITS PAW.

HER STOMACH GAVE A STRANGE FLIP AS SHE FELT HERSELF BEING LIFTED FULLY FROM THE GROUND. SHE WAS BEING CARRIED. SHE FELT THE DRAGON'S LARGE TALON BENEATH HER, CUTTING INTO HER BACK AS HE SEEMED TO GRASP HER FULLY IN HIS CLAWS.
SHE LOOKED DOWN AS THEY PASSED OVER THE LARGE, COUNTRY MANOR WHERE SHE NOW LIVED AND SOARED TO A SPOT NEAR THE BACK OF THE HOUSE. AWAY FROM THE CASTLE AND AWAY FROM THE OTHER CREATURES.

ALANA'S FIRST INSTINCT AS SHE LAY THERE IN THIS ANIMAL'S GRASP WAS TO CALL FOR HELP. BUT, SHE HAD NO VOICE TO DO SO. AND, BESIDES, THERE WAS NO ONE TO HEAR HER BUT THE OTHER DRAGONS SHE HAD SEEN.

As the beast carrying her began to slow his flight, she noticed that they were reaching the ground. When they hit the grass behind the manor with a large thump, Alana gave a gasp of surprised as she was released from her hold and tumbled down onto the grass below.

The creature turned away from her and moved to a spot just a few feet left. She watched as it closed its eyes and slowly, began to shift. A minute later, she saw Llewellyn standing before her breathing heavily as though he had just run a great distance and clutching his side.

Alana stood, staring at him, unsure of what to say. Still unsure that she would be able to say anything at all, even if she tried.
Finally, he looked up at her. He gave her a dark glare which she had never seen from him and marched towards her, his face set. For the first time, she was afraid of him.

He grabbed her none too gently by the wrist and pulled her into the back door of the house. Once inside, they

MOVED TO THE STAIRWELL BEFORE HE GRASPED HER SHOULDERS AND PUSHED HER ROUGHLY AGAINST THE WALL.

"WHAT THE HELL DID YOU THINK YOU WERE DOING?" HE ASKED FIERCELY. LLEWELLYN COULD FEEL HIS HEART POUNDING. HE WAS NOT SURE IF IT WAS ANGER, FEAR FOR ALANA, THE PAIN OF THE SHIFT OR A STRANGE COMBINATION OF ALL THREE.

"WHAT—WHAT WAS THAT? WHAT ARE—"

"YOU REALIZE YOU COULD HAVE DIED," LLEW SAID. IGNORING ALANA'S SHOCKED STAMMERS "IF ANYONE BUT ME HAD SEEN YOU FIRST, YOU WOULD HAVE BEEN KILLED WITHIN TWO MINUTES OR WORSE."

"HOW CAN YOU…YOU CAN SHIFT," ALANA SAID FINALLY. SOUNDING ODDLY TRIUMPHANT THOUGH STILL MORE THAN A BIT BREATHLESS, "I…I MEAN YOU CAN CHANGE INTO—"

"INTO A DRAGON, YES," LLEWELLYN SAID RELUCTANTLY WITH MORE THAN A TRACE OF ANNOYANCE LINING HIS VOICE.

"WHEN WERE YOU PLANNING ON TELLING ME THAT?" ALANA DEMANDED.

"WHEN YOU WERE READY," LLEW SAID.

"YOU WEREN'T YET. YOU SHOULD HAVE WAITED."

"IF YOU HAD TOLD ME THE TRUTH FROM THE BEGINNING, I WOULDN'T HAVE HAD TO," SHE SAID AS FIRMLY AS SHE COULD, THOUGH HER VOICE STILL SHOOK MORE THAN A BIT. HE TOOK HIS HANDS FROM HER SHOULDERS AND RAN ONE HAND OVER HIS FACE, LOOKING AROUND THE ABANDONED STAIRWELL AS THOUGH HOPING SOMEONE MIGHT APPEAR AND TELL HIM WHAT TO DO NEXT. TRUTH BE TOLD, HE WISHED HIS FATHER WERE HERE TO GIVE HIM THE ADVICE HE SO DESPERATELY NEEDED. BUT, HE KNEW THAT, WITH HIS FATHER GONE, HE WOULD HAVE TO MAKE THESE DECISIONS FOR HIMSELF.

"ARE YOU GOING TO TELL ME THE WHOLE TRUTH NOW?" ALANA ASKED. WHEN LLEWELLYN TURNED BACK TO HER, HE SAW HER FACE SET WITH A HARD GLARE. THOSE HAZEL EYES, USUALLY SO WIDE AND INNOCENT WERE NOW LACED WITH A FIRM SET RESOLVE. SHE CLEARLY WOULD NOT ACCEPT ANYTHING BUT THE WHOLE TRUTH FROM HIM NOW.

"YES," HE SAID FINALLY, RELUCTANTLY. ALANA FELT HER EYES WIDEN IN SURPRISE. SHE HAD EXPECTED HIM TO PUT UP ANOTHER FIGHT.

"BUT NOT HERE," HE SAID. HE LIFTED A HAND TO HER CHEEK. SHE WINCED WHEN HIS THUMB RAN OVER A SMALL CUT THAT A JAGGED ROCK HAD GIVEN HER WHEN SHE HAD FIRST PUSHED HERSELF TO THE GROUND.

"I'LL NEED TO TAKE A LOOK AT THAT CUT," HE SAID. "WE'LL GO BACK UP TO YOUR ROOM. I'LL EXPLAIN EVERYTHING THERE."

ALANA ALLOWED HERSELF TO BE LED UP THE DARK, WINDING STAIRWELL, BACK INTO HER LARGE BEDROOM. LLEW OPENED THE DOOR AND PLACED A HAND ON THE SMALL OF HER BACK TO GUIDE HER INSIDE. SHE SHIVERED AT THE WARMTH OF HIS TOUCH THROUGH THE THIN FABRIC OF HER SUMMER DRESS.

FOR HIS PART, LLEW FELT A SMALL AMOUNT OF BLOOD SURGE THROUGH HIM AT EVEN THE SMALLEST TOUCH OF THIS YOUNG AREFOL GIRL. HE WAS CERTAIN NO DRAIG HAD EVER INSPIRED SUCH A FEELING IN HIM AS ALANA DID. IN FACT, HE WAS CERTAIN NO WOMAN, DRAIG OR NOT, HAD CAUSED HIS BODY TO RESPOND THIS WAY.
HE'D FELT IT FIRST WHEN HE'D SEEN HER AT THE BAR. HE REMEMBERED THE MOMENT VIVIDLY. HER LONG DARK HAIR FALLING INTO HER DARK EYES, THE TANTALIZING V-NECK

TOP SHE WORE THAT DISPLAYED A HINT OF CREAMY CLEAVAGE. EVEN THE SLIGHTLY LOST EXPRESSION SHE HAD WORN THAT NIGHT, AS THOUGH SHE WAS OUT OF HER ELEMENT AND LOOKING FOR A PATH BACK HOME, CALLED OUT TO THE BEAST IN HIM MORE THAN ANYTHING ELSE HE COULD REMEMBER.

AND NOW, AS HE SAT HER DOWN ON THE WINDOW SEAT, THE LIGHT FROM THE SUN SHINING ON HER HAIR, THE PALE BLUE SUN DRESS MAKING HER PALE SKIN GLOW AS THOUGH BEGGING TO BE TOUCHED, HE KNEW THAT THIS GIRL WAS DANGEROUS. HE COULD NOT TAKE HER, HE REALIZED THAT. BUT, OH, HOW HE WANTED TO.

INSTEAD OF ACTING ON THIS URGE, HE FOUND A SMALL RAG FROM ONE OF THE CUPBOARDS, DABBED IT WITH RUBBING ALCOHOL AND TOUCHED IT TO HER CHEEK. "THIS WILL STING," HE WARNED.

ALANA LET OUT A SMALL GASP OF PAIN WHEN THE LIQUID TOUCHED HER SKIN BUT GRITTED HER TEETH AGAINST IT UNTIL HE REMOVED THE CLOTH FOR A MOMENT.

"ARE YOU GOING TO TELL ME?" SHE ASKED AS FIRMLY AS SHE COULD WHEN HE WAS SO CLOSE TO HER. HIS BREATH ALMOST TICKLING

HER CHEEK AS HE APPLIED HIS MEDICINE.

HER HEART NEARLY FELL IN DISAPPOINTMENT WHEN HE SAT BACK AND HEAVED A SIGH. SLOWLY, HE BEGAN HIS STORY.

LLEWELLYN TOLD ALANA THAT THE DRAGONS OF WALES WERE NOT A MYTH BUT, RATHER, AN ANCIENT CLAN IN THE REGION. THEY WERE HUNTED TO NEAR EXTINCTION IN THE EARLY ROMAN CENTURIES AND HAD SINCE COMMITTED THEMSELVES TO LIVING IN SECRECY.

"SO, THERE ARE MORE OF YOU?" ALANA ASKED.

"YES," LLEWELLYN SAID. "BUT, NOT MANY NOW. THERE ARE TWO MORE SMALL VILLAGES OF DRAIG'S NEAR SNOWDONIA. AND THERE'S A SMALL COMMUNITY IN CARDIFF. THAT IS WHY MY BROTHER AND I WENT THERE LAST NIGHT. WE WERE...SEARCHING FOR GIRLS WHO MIGHT HELP US."

"IS THAT WHY YOU BROUGHT ME HERE?"

RELUCTANTLY, LLEWELLYN NODDED. HE KNEW HE COULD NOT TELL ALANA THE WHOLE TRUTH. NOT YET. SHE HAD SEEN TOO MUCH THAT DAY.

"OUR CLAN IS DYING OUT," HE EXPLAINED. "BECAUSE WE LIVE IN SECRET, WE'VE BEEN INTERMARRYING FOR YEARS. IT'S NOT SUSTAINABLE. NOW, THERE ARE VERY FEW WOMEN LEFT IN THE CLAN. THE ONES WHO ARE WITH US ARE MATED ALL READY. WHEN MY FATHER, THE CLAN LEADER DIED, HE ASKED ME AND MY BROTHER TO GO TO CARDIFF IN ORDER TO FIND A…A GIRL WHO COULD HELP US."

"HOW, EXACTLY, WAS A GIRL SUPPOSED TO HELP?" ALANA ASKED SUSPICIOUSLY. SHE REMEMBERED LLEW'S BROTHER, OWAIN, GETTING UPSET WITH LLEW FOR BRINGING ALANA. SHE REMEMBERED THAT IT WAS BECAUSE SHE WAS AN "AREFOL". GIVEN THIS INFORMATION, SHE TOOK THAT TO MEAN SIMPLY A 'NONSHIFTER'.

"THERE'S A RITUAL," LLEWELLYN SAID HESITANTLY. "IT TAKES PLACE AT THE FULL MOON. A VIRGIN IS NEEDED TO PERFORM IT."

"WHAT HAPPENS AT THIS…RITUAL?" ALANA ASKED NERVOUSLY.

LLEWELLYN LOOKED AT HER WIDE EYES AND FELT A STAB OF GUILT WHEN HE REALIZED THEY WERE FILLED WITH FEAR. HE KNEW HE NEEDED TO REASSURE HER. EVEN IF

THE PLATITUDES HE OFFERED PROVED UNTRUE.

"NOTHING YOU SHOULD BE FRIGHTENED OF," HE SAID FINALLY. "ANYWAY, IT'S FOUR WEEKS UNTIL THEN. YOU SHOULDN'T WORRY ABOUT IT NOW."

HE PLACED THE ALCOHOL LADEN RAG ON HER CHEEK ONCE MORE. THIS TIME, SHE DIDN'T WINCE. INSTEAD, SHE LOOKED INTO HIS EYES, HALF HOPING AND HALF DREADING WHAT SHE HAD SEEN THERE THE NIGHT BEFORE. THE FLASHING MOVING CREATURE BEHIND THEM. THE BEAST BEHIND THE MAN.

NOW, THERE WAS NONE OF THAT. THERE WAS NO BEAST, NO ANIMAL; NOTHING BUT A MAN LOOKING BACK AT HER, TENDING TO HER CUT WITH MORE TENDERNESS THAN SHE HAD FELT FROM ANY MAN BEFORE.

"I SUPPOSE I SHOULD THANK YOU," SHE SAID QUIETLY. HE STOPPED RUNNING THE CLOTH OVER HER STILL BLEEDING CUT AND LOOKED DIRECTLY AT HER. "AFTER ALL, YOU DID SAVE MY LIFE."

SHE GAVE HIM A SMALL SHY SMILE AND LLEWELLYN COULD SEE A HINT OF COLOR ENTER THE GIRL'S CHEEK. AT THAT LOOK, THAT ONE INNOCENT LOOK, HE FELT HIS RESTRAINT CRUMBLE.

"I WOULD DO IT AGAIN," HE SAID QUIETLY.

THEN, WITHOUT THINKING, WITHOUT WAITING FOR HIS BETTER JUDGMENT TO PROTEST, HE PUT HIS HAND AGAINST HER CHEEK, LEANED FORWARD AND KISSED HER.

IT WAS SOFT, GENTLE, ALMOST UNSURE AT FIRST. BUT, AS ALANA BEGAN TO OPEN TO HIM, WHEN SHE PRESSED BACK AGAINST HIM, LLEW FELT HIS RESTRAINT BREAK APART COMPLETELY.

SOON, HIS HANDS WERE NESTLED IN HER LONG BLACK HAIR AS HE PRESSED HER BACK PASSIONATELY AGAINST THE WINDOW. WHEN SHE PRESSED HERSELF INTO HIM, HE LET OUT A GUTTURAL GROAN AS HE FELT HIS MEMBER BEGIN TO SWELL.

FINALLY, AFTER WHAT SEEMED LIKE AGES BUT, WAS TRULY LESS THAN A DAY, HE WAS TOUCHING HER. KISSING HER, FEELING HER LONG, SOFT HAIR BENEATH HIS FINGERTIPS. SHE LET OUT A SWEET, LITTLE SOUND IN THE BACK OF HER THROAT AS LLEWELLYN FELT A TINY HAND MOVE TO RUN DOWN HIS NAKED TORSO. MORE BLOOD DRAINED FROM HIS HEAD TO HIS GROIN AS SHE CARESSED HIM. SHE WRAPPED HER ARMS AROUND HIM PULLING HIM MORE TIGHTLY TO HER.

IT WAS ONLY WHEN ONE SMALL, DELICATE HAND MOVED TO UNDO THE GOLD BUTTON ON HIS PANTS THAT REALITY RETURNED TO HIM LIKE A SPLASH OF ICE-COLD WATER. THIS GIRL COULD NOT BE HIS MATE. NOT YET.

RELUCTANTLY, HE REMOVED ONE HAND FROM HER HAIR AND TOOK THE HAND THAT WAS SLOWLY UNDOING HIS TROUSER BUTTON BY THE WRIST. STOPPING ITS MOVEMENT.

"WE CAN'T," HE SAID QUIETLY.

"WHY NOT?" SHE ASKED. HER HAZEL EYES LOOKED AT HIM AND HE COULD SEE A MIXTURE OF CONFUSION, PASSION AND A HINT OF HURT LINE HER EXPRESSION.

"I'LL EXPLAIN WHEN I CAN," HE SAID QUICKLY STANDING UP. "I'LL BE BACK IN AN HOUR TO BRING YOU YOUR LUNCH."

WITH THAT, HE HURRIED FROM THE ROOM LEAVING ALANA, CONFUSED AND STILL AROUSED, STARING AFTER HIM.

www.ingramcontent.com/pod-product-compliance
Lightning Source LLC
LaVergne TN
LVHW092101060526
838201LV00047B/1499